The Adventures of
JUSTIN
the Earthman
Superhero Pollution
Crime Fighter

Just Look Up

John W. Waffle

AuthorHouse™
1663 Liberty Drive
Bloomington, IN 47403
www.authorhouse.com
Phone: 1 (800) 839-8640

Published by AuthorHouse 01/21/2015

ISBN: 978-1-4969-6506-6 (sc)
ISBN: 978-1-4969-6507-3 (e)

Library of Congress Control Number: 2015900951

*Any people depicted in stock imagery provided by Thinkstock are models,
and such images are being used for illustrative purposes only.
Certain stock imagery © Thinkstock.*

This book is printed on acid-free paper.

*Because of the dynamic nature of the Internet, any web addresses or links contained in this book may have changed
since publication and may no longer be valid. The views expressed in this work are solely those of the author and do not
necessarily reflect the views of the publisher, and the publisher hereby disclaims any responsibility for them.*

authorHOUSE®

The Adventures of JUSTIN the EARTHMAN Superhero Pollution Crime Fighter

A Day at the Beach

John W. Waffles

Adrian D. Thomas

Illustrations by Cliff Hamilton

Look up in the sky, through the air,
across the land, and over the ocean.

Have no fear, Justin the Earthman is *here!*

Justin is here for *everyone!*

He wants to help us stop pollution
so we can save the *earth!*

Remember . . . help Justin and *don't pollute!*

So we all can say, *Just look up—it's beautiful!*

"Hi, I'm Justin the Earthman. I'm a superhero pollution crime fighter. Can you help me to name some different types of pollutions?"

Air pollution

Light pollution

Noise pollution

Land pollution

Water pollution

Keep thinking. There are lots more. Justin the Earthman needs to know all of them so he can help us keep the earth beautiful and clean.

A Day at the Beach

VOLUME 1

One hot summer day in a place called Littletown, where children live, laugh, dance, and love to play all day, two little children, Johnny and Jodi, needed to cool off from playing their outdoor games.

Johnny said to Jodi, "Hey, Jodi, let's go to one of our favorite fun places—the beach!"

"Oh, yes! It's a great day for the beach!" said Jodi.

"We can go surfing," said Johnny.

"Oh boy, that sounds like fun!" said Jodi. She was cheerful and excited.

With smiles on their faces as bright as the sunshine, Johnny and Jodi arrived at the beach. As they got closer and closer to the waves, all they could say was, "Wow!" They were so excited.

"Look, Johnny! Look at those big, beautiful waves!" said Jodi.

"This is going to be so much fun. Let's get ready to go surfing!" said Johnny.

As Johnny and Jodi ran closer to the ocean waves, carrying their pin-striped surfboards, Johnny began to look frightened. "H–h–hold on, Jodi" he said with a shaky voice. "What is that on the tops of the waves?"

"Oh no!" said Jodi. "It's empty soda bottles and candy wrappers."

"What do we do now?" asked Johnny. His voice was loud; he was upset and worried. Suddenly their smiles turned upside down.

Then, out of nowhere, Justin the Earthman appeared. He spoke in a loud, thundering voice. "I am Justin the Earthman Superhero Pollution Crime Fighter! I am here to help clean up those big, dirty waves. Have no fear! I'm here to turn your frowns back around for you, Johnny and Jodi."

Suddenly, Justin winked and shouted the magical word: "Pollution!" Out popped his super-duper cleaner-upper. Then with a second wink, he again shouted the magical word, "Pollution!" Suddenly, out on top of the mighty big, dirty waves, his solar-powered, super-duper, bright-blue-and-green Jet Ski appeared.

"Whoa!" said Johnny and Jodi.

Justin was now ready for his pollution-crime-fighting mission. He was hoping he could find the ocean villain who had left all the litter in the ocean waves. He needed to find the villain before it was too late. Without a second thought, Justin jumped on his solar-powered, super-duper Jet Ski. He zoomed around and around, up and down, and over and under the waves looking for the ocean villain.

Way down in the deepest part of the ocean, Justin spotted the ocean villain. It was Otto the Octopus. He was laughing, eating, drinking, and talking to his aquatic friends. At the same time he was throwing his candy wrappers and his empty soda bottles into the ocean waves.

Justin the Earthman Superhero Pollution Crime Fighter jumped off of his Jet Ski and shouted, "Otto! You must stop throwing those empty soda bottles and candy wrappers into the ocean waves!"

Justin began to teach Otto a very good lesson about what not to do in the ocean anymore. "Otto, what you are doing is called littering. All that trash is pollution! Your aquatic friends will not like you if you keep polluting their ocean. Otto, please stop. Johnny and Jodi cannot go surfing because of the mess you have left."

Justin and Otto jumped together onto the solar-powered, super-duper Jet Ski. Slowly they began to scoop up all the litter in the ocean waves. At the same time, the magical super-duper cleaner-upper was blowing cleaning bubbles to shine the ocean waves.

27

Little by little, Otto's litter began to disappear. The ocean became bright blue once again. "Without the candy wrappers and the empty soda bottles, the ocean is so beautiful!" said Justin.

With a smile on his face, Otto said, "Yes! You are so right. The ocean *is* beautiful without my candy wrappers and empty soda bottles."

29

"Hooray for the blue and green!" Justin shouted.

"They are the earth's favorite colors!" Otto shouted.

They had won the candy wrapper and the empty soda bottle pollution mission! "It's a great day to be a superhero pollution crime fighter," said Justin.

"And you taught me a very valuable lesson," said Otto. "Thank you."

"Yes, you are welcome, Otto," said Justin. "Maybe someday you can be a superhero pollution crime fighter too!"

Justin sat on his super-duper, blue-and-green Jet Ski high on top of the blue, sparkling, shiny waves. As he searched for another pollution mission to conquer, he looked at the shore and saw Johnny and Jodi with smiles on their faces.

Johnny looked at Jodi, and Jodi looked at Johnny. With newfound enthusiasm, they both ran across the hot, sandy beach with their pin-striped surfboards held tightly in their arms. Johnny yelled, "One, two, three!" And into the waves they went with their groovy surfboards. Soon they were rocking and rolling on the big, bright, sparkling, shiny blue waves.

Now Justin truly knew that Johnny and Jodi were enjoying the hot, beautiful, bright, sunny day.

As the sun began to go down, it was time for Johnny and Jodi to go home. They were both very, very tired. They'd had so much fun surfing, and they couldn't wait to do it again the next day.

As for Otto the Octopus, he is no longer a litterbug. He is now teaching Stan the Starfish, Sam the Clam, and Boris the Seahorse not to throw litter into the ocean waves. Now Otto the Octopus rides the ocean waves with brooms and buckets hanging from his long, wiggly arms. Every day he helps Justin to continue the never-ending battle against pollution.

As for Justin the Earthman, as magically as he appeared, he disappeared into the big, blue, sparkling waves. But have no fear. He is always near, and ready to go on a new pollution adventure.

So listen everyone to what Justin
says: "Just look up and don't pollute.
Please, just look up—it's beautiful!"

Before he left, Justin sent a kite flying
over the waves to Jodi and Johnny. There
was a note attached to the string.

Dear Johnny and Jodi,

Fly this kite high in the big, beautiful blue sky, and don't forget to pull on the string three times. You will need this for the next new exciting pollution crime adventure!

Sincerely,

Justin the Earthman Superhero
Pollution Crime Fighter!

ABOUT THE AUTHORS

John W. Waffles grew up in a little town outside of Philadelphia, Pennsylvania. He is a graduate of Johnson and Wales University. Mr. Waffles was on the dean's list at university, and after he graduated, he went into the restaurant business and owned several restaurants. Throughout his busy life, Mr. Waffles always had many ideas for stories and the passion to write them. His ideas for writing came and went until one day—on June 10, 2012, to be exact—when he was jogging along an outdoor trail, he glanced up at the big, beautiful sky. He also noticed parents with their happy, smiling, innocent children. Mr. Waffles suddenly stopped jogging and placed a phone call to Mr. Thomas. He said to his friend, "Just look up!" Together they trademarked the phase "Just look up—it's beautiful." They also copyrighted the name Justin the Earthman. Thus began their quest to stop pollution and to help save our planet for our children and their children of tomorrow. "The passion to write and to teach our children about our earth and how not to pollute is now so very strong that I'll never put my pen down again," said Mr. Waffles. "So, remember, let's all glance up at the big beautiful blue sky so we can say, 'Just look up—it's beautiful.' Together with our children, we can keep the earth blue and green!

Adrian D. Thomas currently resides outside of Philadelphia Pennsylvania. A graduate of La Salle University, he has always had a keen sense of environmental concerns. "Being able to address some issues about saving the planet was quite intriguing," he says. "Teaching our children is the start of this process. Hopefully this will lead to a fun and cleaner planet."

ABOUT THE BOOK

The earth is a beautiful and magical planet where all our children live, dance, and play all day. So let's all do our share to help Justin the Earthman keep our planet blue and green! "Just look up—it's beautiful."

Stay tuned! There's a new action-packed Justin the Earthman Superhero Pollution Crime Fighter adventure story coming soon to your favorite online bookstores and your favorite bookstores.

CPSIA information can be obtained at www.ICGtesting.com
Printed in the USA
BVOW11s2329010215

385805BV00004B/6/P

9 781496 965066